MW01234364

Nimbus

A Sentient Object Romance
Nicole Parker

Copyright © 2024 by Nicole Parker

All rights reserved. No part of this publication may be reproduced, stored or transmitted in any form or by any means, electronic, mechanical, photocopying, recording, scanning, or otherwise without written permission from the publisher. It is illegal to copy this book, post it to a website, or distribute it by any other means without permission.

This novel is entirely a work of fiction. The names, characters and incidents portrayed in it are the work of the author's imagination. Any resemblance to actual persons, living or dead, events or localities is entirely coincidental.

This book was written by a human. No part of this book was written using artificial intelligence. I support artists and will never use generative artificial intelligence in my books.

Book Cover by Author

Interior Art by Fanyk

First Edition 2024

Paperback ISBN: 9798333162274

Independently Published

For everyone battling their own storm and the ones who help them weather it.

Content Considerations

First and foremost, this is a sentient object romance which means people will get down and dirty with a sentient object, but everything is consensual.

There is a happy ending, however there are many depictions of anxiety and panic attacks throughout.

In no particular order, there is explicit sex (oral, anal, cloud), cursing, flavored cum, and multiple partners.

If you feel I am missing anything, please reach out and let me know. An updated list can be found at:

http://booksbynicoleparker.com/nimbus

Contents

Prologue

Owen

I'm lying back on a blanket looking up at the clouds in the sky, trying to make out shapes. I do this whenever the world feels like too much. Something about watching them drift across the sky calms me. I notice a dark storm cloud looming in the distance. Looks like rain is coming. Time to pack up my things and head home. To be alone with my thoughts. Again. I focus on deep breaths, trying to keep myself centered.

Suddenly, I sense a woman standing in my peripheral vision. I didn't notice her at first and wonder how long she's been there. Having seen me spot her, she approaches and glances up at the sky. "I like them too." The accent is unique, so it only takes me a moment to confirm her as one of the regulars from work. Herbal tea with 2 honeys. Brittany, I think. She rarely says much, but will spend hours at the cafe reading. Not her cell phone or e-reader like most folks, but big, heavy-looking volumes. I don't say anything and a moment passes before she continues. "The clouds. I like them too."

"Oh, yeah." My hands fidget with the blanket as I look up at the sky. She glances down at my hands, noticing my nervous energy. Self-conscious, I try to stop and hold still.

She smiles, places a hand on my arm, and I immediately feel a sense of calm. It washes over me, emanating from her touch. It's bizarre, like nothing I've ever felt before.

"A nice guy like you deserves someone to help them weather the storm." She glances at the clouds coming in.

"Oh, thank you, but I..." I trail off as I see she has already turned and is walking away, mumbling words that I cannot quite understand. The sense of calm she provided stays with me as I head home, trying to figure out what the hell just happened.

Chapter One

Owen

"Welcome to The Magic Bean. What can I get you today?"

"I'll have a medium, extra hot, non-fat, half-caf, light whip mocha." The woman purses her lips, waiting for me to jot down her order on the cup.

"Anything else today?" I ask with a fake smile. This lady comes in every day, ordering the same ridiculous drink.

"And don't forget to melt the chocolate with the espresso. I don't want it to be all sludgy on the bottom." I continue smiling back. She never orders anything else. I'm not sure she's ever noticed that it's the same person taking her order day after day. She shakes her head and taps her card on the machine before walking to wait at the far end of the counter.

"Good morning, Owen." One of our more pleasant regulars, Chloe, walks up next with her arm wrapped around her new boyfriend, Garrett.

"Morning, Chloe. Morning, Garrett. The usual?"

She smiles. "Yep. Oh, and I'm picking up Kyle's too. Thanks." I note Chloe's hazelnut latte and Garrett's double espresso, pour Kyle's black coffee myself, and hand it over the counter to her. I watch as the happy couple turns and walks away, but an impatient cough draws my attention back to the next customer.

The morning goes by quickly until the before-work rush slows to a trickle. Ironically, it's the slow times that give me the most trouble. As long as I keep busy, I don't have time for my mind to wander or worry about things, but the moment I have a minute to myself, I can feel my anxiety creep in. Being surrounded by unlimited amounts of caffeine probably doesn't help.

I do all the tasks the other employees try to put off, solely because I can't sit still. It makes me a good employee, I guess. I'm outside cleaning the patio tables when I feel one of my "the sky is falling" moments coming on. It's what I call the times something trivial happens that triggers an unreasonably huge cascade of negative emotions. Today, I knocked over a napkin dispenser, popping it open and causing the napkins to spill everywhere. A breeze then picked up the napkins, scattering them all down the street. I chased after like an idiot, trying to pick up as many as I could. Before I knew it, I was spiraling, thinking about the amount of litter I had created which led to the general concept of pollution which led to the state of the planet and how the world was probably going to end in my lifetime. The rational side of my brain realizes that my spilling a handful of napkins will probably not directly contribute to the death of the planet, but once my thoughts start to snowball, the rational side of my brain checks out.

Breathing heavily, I tuck myself into the alleyway behind the shop, sit down, put my head between my knees, and try to focus on the grounding exercises my therapist suggested. I try to go through my 5 senses. First, five things I can see. *I see the alley concrete, a lonely ant walking by, the big dumpsters, my converses which need to be re-tied, and the brick wall of the building.* Next, four things I can hear. *I hear the cars driving by, someone talking loudly on their cell phone, a dog barking, and some kind of bird.* I'm focusing on three things I can touch when I notice a thick fog has surrounded me. It's been cloudy all morning, like a storm was coming in, but this fog seems unusual. The peculiarity of it pauses my racing thoughts and I lift my head to look around.

I see what looks like someone condensing from the fog itself, but has got to be just walking through the mist in my direction. He has soft, curly hair framing a pleasant round face. He's tall, but nothing about him looks intimidating. In fact, it's the exact opposite. He seems like someone who would wrap you up in the best hug.

He glances down at me, then around at the alleyway. "What's going on?"

Oh, you know, having a little panic attack here. I'm unsure what to say to this stranger. I'm not even sure whether I'm going to answer at all when he walks over and sits next to me, matching my position, hugging his knees to his chest. Even sitting curled up, this guy is still nearly a head taller than me. Everything about him seems larger than life.

I blow out a breath, letting my head fall back to rest against the brick wall behind me, and look up at the sliver of sky between the buildings. The grey storm clouds seem to have completely disappeared, leaving only a clear blue sky with a few bright white puffs. "You ever feel like the sky is falling?" When he doesn't answer, I rock my head to the side to look at him. He is also staring upward now with a smile I can't quite read. I look back up, watching the clouds move and change above me, noting some of the shapes I find. I don't even realize how long I zone out, but when I turn to look back at the stranger again, he's gone.

Chapter Two

Gale

Well, that was sure something. One second, I'm happily floating along, pouring rain along my path. The next I'm standing in an alleyway with a beautiful guy. Beautiful, but sad. He looked so helpless, sitting there all curled up, his long brown hair covering his eyes. I couldn't even see that they were green (my favorite color) until he looked up and saw me, the red from crying making them stand out even more.

Do I ever feel like the sky is falling? More like I feel like I'm falling from the sky. I don't know how he pulled me to him or why. The poor guy looked like he needed a friend, but I would assume he's got plenty.

Before I could figure out what the hell was happening, I was back up in the sky, doing what I do best. Not everybody appreciates a good thunderstorm, but I get the feeling the guy in the alley would.

I spend the next week staying overhead, watching him go about his life. It's not possible to stay much longer without drawing the attention of the local meteorologists, but I don't think I can move on either. I need to know what happened that brought me to that alley with him. I want to make it happen again.

Chapter Three
Owen

It's rained all week, but I've been working so much that I haven't been able to go outside and enjoy it. The grey weather seems to be driving everyone into the cafe, wanting hot coffee to warm them up when all I want is to get out of here. I'm having yet another day where nothing seems to go right. I burn my hand on the steam wand, which causes me to spill milk everywhere. Then I bump my head while standing up from sopping up all that spilled milk and feel just about ready to break down when I hear the voice that's haunted me this past week.

"Any chance you're hiring?"

I pop my head up, hand still rubbing the bump on the back of my head, and sure enough, it's my mystery stranger. I haven't seen him since that day in the alley, but I haven't been able to get him out of my head since. For some reason, each time I look up and see the storm clouds in the sky, I think of him.

He's looking at me with a smile that seems to light up his entire face. I can't help but smile back at him.

"Is your head OK? That looks like it hurt."

Suddenly embarrassed, I pull my hand down to my side. "We're not at the moment. Umm... hiring, I mean." My coworker, Mollie, jabs me in the ribs and shoots me a look. "OK, maybe we could use a little extra help." I shoot her a look back. "But I'm not sure how many hours we'd be able to give you."

"That sounds great. Whatever you have is fine."

He stands there for another beat, just smiling and looking into my eyes. Mollie clears her throat and hands him an application.

"Oh, right. We'll need you to fill this out."

He looks it over and blushes a little. "Some of this will be, ah, a little hard for me to fill out. I don't exactly have a permanent address."

He doesn't have a place to live? I give Mollie a worried glance. We need the application on file to hire him and, for reasons I'm not ready to admit, it's important to me that he is hired. I blurt out, without really thinking, "You can use my address." Mollie looks at me with surprise, raising an eyebrow, but says nothing as she returns to the bar and starts making drinks, pretending to ignore whatever is going on with the application. "We need an address for your file, but everything is electronic anyway, so the address doesn't really matter." I can feel the red creeping up my cheeks.

He smiles and spins the application to me so that I can enter my information. I hastily scribble my address before turning it back to him. He fills out a few more boxes before finishing and handing it back to me. There are a few blank spots remaining, but I think it's enough to move forward. I look over the application and notice that he's watching me again.

"I should interview you." I give a nervous laugh as he continues beaming that smile at me. With anyone else I would find this super creepy, but with him I feel warm, seen. I gesture to one of the empty tables in the corner. We sit down, facing one another. His legs are so long and the table so small that his feet end up extended under my chair. "OK. It says here your name is Gale. My name is Owen." I look up at him again. His eyes are a stormy grey, making me think of the rain we've been having. I stare for a few seconds too long before glancing back down at the application. We don't have any standard interview questions and there's no way I'm not making sure he gets hired, so this entire interview is pointless, but I want to spend more time talking with him. "Where did you go the other day?"

He chuckles. "Is that an interview question?"

"Oh, um, no. I was watching the clouds and then you were gone."

"Do you do that often?"

"What?" Get flustered in the presence of attractive men? Yes.

"Watch the clouds?"

"Yeah." I smile. "Since I was a kid. Watching the clouds has always helped me feel calmer." The thought seems to make him happy, the corners of his mouth turning up slightly. "Did you not do that as a kid?"

"I wouldn't say I find watching clouds to be particularly relaxing. I've always preferred people-watching."

"Were you watching me last week?" The words come out in a whisper. The thought of this man watching me have a complete breakdown almost triggers another.

He must see the panic in my eyes. He grabs my hand, rubbing circles with his thumb, then glances around the coffee shop. "This probably isn't appropriate talk for an interview." He smiles at me but doesn't let go of my hand.

I huff out a laugh. "Of course. You're right. It was inappropriate for me to bring it up. Sorry." I pull my hand back, picking up the application and staring at it, although my brain can no longer process the words. "I'll pass this on to management and they'll contact you."

He smiles, shakes my hand politely, and heads towards the door.

"Gale?"

He turns back to look at me as I walk to him. This is insane and may be how I end up murdered. "I don't know your situation, but if you're between places, you can stay with me. The couch pulls out."

He grins. "I think I'd like that."

I jot down the address for him again and let him know when I'll be home so he can meet me there. He gives a little wave to Mollie as he walks out the door. I watch as he walks down the street, where I swear he dissolves into the fog, but it must be my eyes playing tricks on me again.

Chapter Four
Gale

I float back up into the sky. That was stupid, Gale. I don't even know why I'm getting pulled down to see Owen, but now I've agreed to move in with him? How the hell am I going to make that work?

The first thing I need to figure out is how to get back down to him on the ground. I focus my energy on bringing myself down to the surface, but nothing happens. I release a bolt of lightning in frustration. Changing doesn't seem to be something I can manage by will, so Owen must be causing it somehow, which means there's no way I can make it happen on my own.

I picture Owen at his home waiting for me, assuming I've stood him up, and rain starts pouring down hard. Why would I agree to this? I was lucky enough to get pulled down to see him again today. I don't know why I pretended I needed a job or a place to live. It just seemed like the easiest way to continue talking to him.

I need to figure out a way to signal him, to let him know that I'm not standing him up. Well, technically I am, but not because I want to.

I watch as he leaves work and attempt to get his attention by dropping copious amounts of rain, but I realize there's no way he would understand that. He has no idea I am a cloud and a little extra rain means nothing to him, other than maybe he needs an umbrella. He looks up at the sky for a second and I swear his eyes linger on me.

He said he enjoys watching clouds. I wonder what he thinks of looking at me. I watch a smile form on his lips before he raises his umbrella and begins his journey home. He makes it to his destination safely, and now I assume he's inside, waiting for me to arrive. Little does he know I'm waiting right outside his door with no way to get in.

Chapter Five

Owen

My palms are actually sweaty as I unlock the door to my apartment. I don't see Gale anywhere, but he could be here any minute. I glance around my small home. It's not spotless, but it's not a disaster either. I perform a haphazard 5-minute clean and ensure there's nothing too gross about my living situation.

This was such a mistake! This guy could be a fucking serial killer and I gave him my home address and basically told him I would be alone tonight if he wanted to off me. Shit. What was I thinking? I feel my heart racing, panic setting in when I hear a knock at my door. I consider crumpling to the floor in the spot I stand and simply ignoring it, but there are more knocks, sounding forceful. It's Gale.

"Owen, are you alright?" Despite being muffled through the closed front door, I can hear genuine concern in his voice. I try to slow down my breathing. I wipe my eyes and stand, figuring I may as well let him in. He already saw me having a panic attack the other day.

I open the door and take in the sight of Gale. His bulk fills the door frame. His eyes are concerned and searching. He's not carrying anything with him, which I find odd, but I can't deal with processing that at the moment. He's changed into a more casual outfit, wearing sweats and a t-shirt, both of which do too good of a job clinging to his body. The t-shirt strains against his enormous broad chest. The sweatpants hug his thighs and nicely accentuate an ample bulge up front. I can only imagine what his ass looks like.

"Can I come in?" He smiles at me nervously.

"Oh, yeah, of course." My mind snaps back into the present, feelings of panic seeming distant now. I move out of the doorway as Gale enters, looking around. "Sorry, the tour's not very impressive, but the kitchen's over there, the bathroom's over there. My room's there. And, uh, this is the couch." I gesture towards it. "Like I said, it's a pullout." I look up and down at the giant man before me. The couch suddenly looks way too tiny. Maybe I should offer him my bed?

"I really appreciate this." He takes a step closer to me.

"Yeah, sure, it's no problem."

"I don't want to take advantage of your hospitality, so let me know if I overstay my welcome." He's so close to me now that I need to crane my neck to look up at him. I nod, unable to form coherent thoughts. His eyes glance down at mine and then my lips for a brief second. I swallow, wondering if he's going to make a move, but he breaks away, turning to walk to the couch. I let out a breath, disappointed.

"Would you like anything? Maybe a snack or something to drink?"

"Water would be great." I run to the kitchen and fill a glass of water, which he gulps down in a large swallow. I wonder whether I should refill the glass or give him space to settle in when he reaches out to take my hand and pulls me down onto the couch beside him. He turns his body to face me, placing one arm behind me on the couch. "You overthink every decision you make." He says it like a statement, so I don't respond. "Yet you invited me to stay here. Why?"

My eyes go wide. It's the same question I've been asking myself, and I don't know the answer. I look down at my feet and wring my hands, trying to come up with some kind of reasonable response. His large thumb and forefinger grab my chin, directing my face to look up at him. Once my eyes are on his, I feel his hand slide gently across my jaw, down my neck, over my shoulder, and down my arm until he holds my small hand in his large one. His touch is electric. It feels like my skin is prickling every place he contacted. My cock grows hard, pushing against the zipper of my pants. If I'm honest, that's the real reason I invited him here. I can hardly admit it to myself, though; I'm not usually the forward one. His thumb rubs circles against my hand. It feels like the nerves there are on fire. I stare into his deep grey eyes. He must know the answer already. Why is he making me say it?

"I..." I start, but can't get the words out. The hand on the back of the couch moves to grab the back of my neck, squeezing firmly.

He leans in a little closer. "Tell me, Owen."

"I... I want you," I whisper.

He releases my hand from his grip, his forearm coming to rest on my leg as he leans in close and brings his mouth to my ear. "You want me to what?" I feel his fingertips slowly teasing around the outside of my thigh. His hand slowly moves up, stopping right before reaching the spot I want it to. He uses his powerful hands on my neck and groin to keep me held where he wants me. His eyes bore into mine, probing for an answer. "You want me to what, Owen?" I can't look away from his gaze, but I also cannot say what I feel out loud, so I try to avoid the question by reaching forward with my hand, palming his dick.

He lets out a hiss. The next thing I know, he grabs my wrist, turns me, and pins me down on the couch, one arm above my head. He slowly grabs the other and brings it up, trapping both my arms easily in one of his massive hands. Gale pauses briefly to search my eyes, but finding no hesitation, he continues. He positions my hips and legs together on the couch so that he can straddle me comfortably. As he settles his weight down on top of me, I can't help but thrust into him. I'm going to fucking come in my pants if he keeps this up. He grins and puts a little more of his weight onto me, pinning me down fully. I'm helplessly trapped.

He leans forward and breathes in my ear. "You want to stop this any time? We stop, OK?" He pulls back and looks at me. I nod. "Not using your words got you into this, coffee boy. Say you understand."

I lick my lips, considering being a brat and not answering. I'm not upset about where we are right now, but I get the idea he's not moving things forward without my verbal consent. "I understand."

"Good boy." He grins. "But I still owe you some punishment. You don't get my cock until I tell you that you can have it. Understand?" I nod my head. He grinds his hips against my cock, causing me to moan.

"Yes, I understand!"

"Tell me what you want, coffee boy." He rocks his hips again. We haven't even taken off any clothing and I'm already losing it. He kisses my neck, the sensitive skin tingling.

"Please."

"Please what?" He asks against my neck before swirling his tongue.

"I want your cock. I want to come. I want all of it." I say it all in one breath, hoping it's good enough.

He reaches down, undoing my pants with a quick flip and firmly grabbing my cock, rubbing the bead of pre-cum all over the tip with his large thumb.

"Good boy," he murmurs against my ear. "Show me how you like it." He releases my wrists and grabs my hair as he continues kissing my neck. I move my now free arms between our bodies and wrap my hands over his on my cock, showing him exactly how I like to be touched. "Are you going to come for me, coffee boy?"

"Yes," I grunt out, already so close. After a couple more tugs, I explode, my cum covering both of our shirts. We stay like that, me breathing heavily, him lying on top of me, peppering me with sweet kisses for a few minutes. He kisses my forehead before rolling off me and walking to the bathroom to clean up.

Chapter Six
Gale

Fuck. That was amazing. I stand with my hands on the counter, trying to calm myself down. I was terrified that I would shift back into a cloud at any moment, but thanks to whatever is causing this to happen, I held it together.

I look down at my shirt, currently a mess with Owen's cum. I think the expectation would be to clean up, but it's not like I have other clothes to change into. The shirt and clothes have just kind of appeared with me whenever I've transformed. I haven't given it much thought until this moment.

There's no way I could fit into one of Owen's small shirts. I'd rip them to shreds even attempting to get them over my shoulders. I remove my dirty shirt, deciding I should at least attempt to wash it off some. I turn on the shower to rinse it, without thinking about what all the extra moisture in the air would do to me.

Once the steam hits, I begin to shift back into cloud form, soaking up the moisture in the air. Shit. Shit. Shit. Lightning cracks and thunder rumbles around me before I can stop it. Not only am I going to be stuck in cloud form, but I'm in his apartment, trapped in his only fucking bathroom, with no way out.

I hear a soft knock on the door, but I can't answer. I look around for any solution. There's an overhead fan. I hadn't turned it on when I came in, and I'm not sure where I would wind up if I tried to exit through a vent, but I'm considering it. I realize it's too late as the doorknob turns and I watch in horror.

"Gale? Everything alright in there? Did something get knocked down?" His voice is not much louder than a whisper. He stares at me, confused. I can instantly see the worry in his eyes as his breath hitches.

Somehow, I feel my body rapidly solidify back into my human form. I turn the water off quickly, trying to avoid any more changes. I look down at myself, now entirely dry and wearing new clothes that have magically manifested, standing in a shower where a thundercloud had been only seconds before.

"I can explain." I start. Who am I kidding? I can't explain this. I don't even know why I'm human right now and not a puff of water vapor, but I think I'm getting an idea.

"I brought you a towel, but... umm.... maybe you don't need it?" Looking perplexed, he extends the towel out to me and I take it. It feels like the right thing to do.

"Uh, thank you." I hold Owen's confused gaze as I use the towel to dab my dry face. He nods, looking very uncertain, and backs out of the bathroom without another word.

I stand there, clutching the towel, unsure of what to do next. I slowly tiptoe out into the living room but do not see Owen, instead I find his bedroom door shut tight. When I knock, there's no response.

"Owen, I'm sorry. Look, I'll give you some space, but I would like to try to explain." I rest my head on the door. "Please, let me know when we can talk… if you want to talk."

Chapter Seven

Owen

A cloud jacked me off? The thought repeats over and over in my head as I hug my knees tightly against my chest. *And it felt really good.* He says he can explain, but what is there to explain? He's a fucking cloud person? That's not possible. Forget it.

I hear the door to my apartment open and shut, and after a few minutes, I unlock my bedroom door to peek out to see if he's actually gone. But he's fucking water vapor! Maybe he's just gone invisible. He could probably squeeze through the cracks around my door if he wanted to. Oh my God. He can get to me wherever I am. Oh fuck, what if he's here right now? I can never feel safe again.

I feel my panic level rise. I grab an ice cube from the freezer and clutch it in my fist. Sometimes the sharp cold is enough to shock me out of a spiral. I try to do my grounding exercises at the same time.

Nothing about Gale gave me any indication that I was not safe with him. In fact, from the moment I met him, I've felt *more* safe than ever. Tonight, he went out of his way to make sure I felt comfortable as we progressed. I know he's not going to break into my apartment. He's just not that kind of guy. Cloud. Whatever.

I take a slow, deep breath and look at the puddle forming under my hand. I watch a last drop fall from my balled fist before tossing the remaining bit of ice cube into the sink and grabbing a towel to wipe up the melted ice water from the floor. I start laughing, maybe a bit too hard, at the fact I used one form of water to help me through a panic attack about another form of water.

I shake my head and try to pull myself together before falling down the anxiety rabbit hole any further. What I need is rest. Unfortunately, sleep doesn't come, but my 4:30 alarm does. Opening shift at The Magic Bean.

Somehow I make it to the shop on time, but it's another classic Owen morning when I scald the milk, burn my hand, and drop the pitcher. Frothy milk foam flies everywhere. Mortified, I grab a towel to soak up the mess, but Mollie can tell I need a moment and snaps at me to just go on break. I know she's trying to help me, but all the same I hear her muttering under her breath that it would be easier to do everything herself. She's probably not wrong.

I whip off my stained apron and take a seat on the patio, dropping my head into my hands.

"Well, if it isn't my favorite barista." I look up as one of our regulars, Kyle, pulls out a chair at my table and sits down across from me, waving goodbye to his friend as she walks away. He's sweaty, clearly having just finished a run. His clothes cling to his body, reminding me of my cloud man. I shake my head and refocus on the normal human man in front of me instead of the sexy mist man I pushed away last night.

"I thought Mollie was your favorite." He's constantly flirting with her.

"Whichever of you is making my coffee. Or is within earshot. So right now, that makes you my favorite." He grins at me. I try to smile back, but between the lack of sleep and the fact that a fucking cloud jacked me off, I don't think I pull it off. "Alright. What's going on?"

I huff out a wry laugh. "You wouldn't believe me."

He laughs back in response. "And you wouldn't believe how much I can believe." I raise an eyebrow at him. He holds up his hands. "Listen, Owen, all I'm saying is I've experienced some weird shit. At this point, there's very little I won't at least consider."

"Fine. A cloud jacked me off last night." I blurt out somewhat defiantly, waiting for him to laugh or tell me I'm crazy.

His eyebrows raise, but only slightly. "Oh yeah? Did you have to do it up in the sky, or did they come down for it?" He leans back in his chair, waiting for my response.

"Oh, um, he was a person at the time. I didn't know he was a cloud until after."

Kyle leans forward, steepling his fingers, face pensive. "I see. And you wish he would've told you before he jacked you off?"

"No, I wish he wasn't a cloud!" I say it a bit too loudly, causing pedestrians to look my way.

"Why?" Kyle leans forward as I try to formulate a response. "Is cloud sex not good?"

"No. What? That's not the point. And it was great, thank you."

"Then what *is* the point?"

"You can't go around having sex with clouds," I say without any confidence, feeling utterly confused. Before last night I would've meant it, but now I'm doubting myself.

"If a cloud offered me sex, I'd probably take it." Kyle squints, tilting his head up and looking skyward. "You can let your cloud friend know I'm down in the case you're not." He shrugs. "Or if you were down, but wanted to share..." Kyle's eyes lock on mine as he gives me a mischievous smile. My mouth hangs open as I try to produce words. He breaks his gaze and stands, lazily stretching his back, extending an arm straight up skyward and yawning. He must realize I have no words, so he simply reaches out and squeezes my shoulder. "Owen, if it were me, I'd give your cloud guy a chance." He stands up and heads to the front door of the cafe. "Now, I need to see my other favorite barista about a coffee." I watch him walk inside, thinking through all he just said.

Chapter Eight
Gale

I float high above the ground, keeping an eye on Owen. I told him I wanted to explain, but I'm worried that even if he wanted to contact me, I won't be able to shift to human form to speak with him. And that's my best-case scenario. There is a good chance he won't ever want to talk to me. Maybe I fucked it all up.

I saw him talking to some guy earlier. It surprised me how jealous I became. I could not hear their conversation from way up here, but I could see when the guy touched Owen. I want Owen to be mine. Only mine. I know I have no right to feel this way, but there's something about him that activates a protective instinct in me.

Despite how I feel, I try to stay out of his way, letting the cumulus clouds do their thing. The last thing Owen needs right now is another rainy day. For now, I have to be content to watch him from afar.

I see him leave work and walk to the park. He finds a spot on an open hillside in an uncrowded corner. I watch as he unrolls a blanket and lies down, gazing up at the sky. He told me he enjoyed watching the clouds to relax. He scans the air, eyes glancing past the fluffy white cumulus clouds, until he finds me.

I know I stand out, the dark shadow among the puffy white cotton balls. He sits up, staring at me. He looks down for a second, takes a deep breath, and then looks back up at me, smiles, and nods.

I do everything I can think of to turn back into a person, but nothing works. I can see the confusion on Owen's face and I want to explain to him, but I'm stuck as a fucking cloud. Why did I think this would work? Bolts of lightning flash as I lose control of my emotions.

This isn't fair. Why would any of this happen in the first place if I can't get to him now when I need to most? What was the point of it all? My mind starts to race, I can feel myself unraveling, and I realize I'm having a "sky is falling" moment of my own, when sensation overwhelms me and I am falling from the sky.

Well, maybe not falling, but it is unsettling being high in the atmosphere one moment and then somehow in human form on the ground the next. I look around, trying to find my bearings. The sudden change in perspective is disconcerting. I don't think I am too far from the hillside where Owen is lying on his blanket. I try to walk through the park with some dignity, but instead find myself doing a hurried walk/jog, eager to get there as fast as possible. Luckily, these long human legs can carry me quickly. As I round the next turn in the path, I see him on the hillside, lying on his back and still staring up at the sky. I take a second to appreciate this moment, pausing to take in the sight of him. In case I don't get any opportunities after this, I want to remember it. I walk over to his blanket to take a seat next to him.

"You looked kind of sad up there."

I tilt my head, surprised. I didn't think he'd be able to read my emotions in cloud form. "I was."

He turns to look at me. "Why?"

"I fucked things up last night and then I saw you with someone else today and I couldn't figure out how to get back to you. I had my own 'sky is falling' moment."

He laughs. "I didn't mean that literally." He looks back up at the sky, face becoming serious for a second before a wide smile forms on his face. "The person you saw me with today was Kyle. He is a friend and was trying to help. He actually went so far as offering to fuck you. Or both of us if we wanted. He's... different. But different good. You would like him, I think. "

My mind races through possibilities before it circles back to the bigger point. "You told him about me? About what I am?"

He blows out a breath. "Sorry. Was I not supposed to do that? You never said I couldn't. We never had a chance to talk about it, and I was kind of freaking out a little." He turns to look at me again. "OK, I was freaking out a lot and needed to process. I didn't tell him your name or which cloud you are. I don't know if that matters."

"Well, how did you know which cloud I was?"

He smiles. "It's your eyes. The colors match. Plus, you're the only thundercloud in the sky today - you sort of stand out. But even if there were hundreds of storm clouds, I think I could find you. I don't know, it's still you. I think I saw you last night before you came over, too. Before I really knew." I smile. I knew he was looking straight at me. "Why didn't you tell me?"

"I was planning on it. I was planning on a lot, actually. I didn't intend for things to go as far or as fast as they did. I wanted to tell you before things got physical, but everything started happening, and I got caught up in the moment, and I was so worried I'd get turned back into a cloud, and I didn't want to waste any of our time together." I realize I'm rambling, so I take a breath. "I was scared."

He nods. "Given how I reacted, that makes sense. I'm guessing the others haven't reacted well either?"

"The others?" My brows scrunch together.

"I can't imagine I'm the first person you've... you know." He blushes.

"This has never happened before." Now it's my turn to blush.

He props himself up on an elbow. "But you were so..." He trails off.

I push his hair behind his ear. "I don't know what's going on here. One second I was a cloud and the next I was with you. I can't control it, but I need you to know that if I could, I would choose to be here with you."

He smiles at me. "Well, you seem to conveniently show up whenever I need you most. For now, that's good enough. We can work out more as we figure it out. Together."

Chapter Nine

Owen

I take Gale's hand and together we practically sprint back to my apartment. Kyle was right. Who gives a fuck if he's a cloud? He's sweet and safe and somehow always there for me when I need him to be.

We make it to my apartment out of breath and panting. Our mouths crash together as I fumble with the keys, trying to open the door. It swings open and we stumble through. I nearly lose my balance as I lean into him. I gain my feet and immediately yank off his shirt, my hands frantically roaming his body. He groans as he nearly lifts me off the floor, pushing me towards my room, and playfully throws me onto my bed. He's so fucking strong!

"Stay." I make a show of perfect obedience, freezing in place for him. He quickly rewards me. His pants are off in an instant, his thick cock hard and glistening. I fight the urge to grab it by balling my hands in the comforter. "Good boy," he purrs. He grins at me as he slowly strokes his length, clearly enjoying teasing me. "Are you going to tell me what you want this time, coffee boy?"

I shake my head, eager for whatever punishment he deems suitable.

"So that's how you want to play it, hmm?" I grin back at him. He saunters over to me, stopping right in front of me. He bends toward me slowly before suddenly yanking off my pants with more force than I'm expecting, the friction leaving a burning sensation on my legs. I'm already rock hard and now my cock is on full display. He rubs his hands up my thighs as his huge body looms over me. His cock touches mine and an involuntary twitch jerks through my body. Face close to mine, he whispers in my ear, "On your knees" and abruptly stands back up near the foot of the bed. I nod and start sliding down the bed, dropping to the floor in front of him. He roughly grabs my hair, moving me into position before forcing me to look up at him. "Snap if you need to stop." I nod and grin. "Say it, coffee boy."

"Yeah, yeah. Just give me that cock."

He grunts, shutting me up by slamming his long shaft into my mouth. I gag as the head of his dick finds my throat. He holds me there for a moment as I struggle, but quickly pulls back again, letting me breathe. "Just had to be mouthy, didn't you?" He begins thrusting into my mouth, more slowly this time. "Couldn't just take my dick like a good boy?" I moan against his cock and reach for my own. "No touching, coffee boy. This is a punishment, remember?" I whimper but put my hands around his legs as he picks up the pace, fucking my face now. I relax my throat as I try to allow more of his length inside me. "You feel so fucking good." He continues driving into me. I love the feeling as the head of his cock glides over my tongue. "You're going to take all my cum, aren't you?" There are tears in my eyes as I try to answer, but can only manage grunting noises around his enormous dick. I feel his leg muscles tense and his hands fist in my hair as ropes of cum shoot down my throat. He tries to pull back, but I hold him firmly in place and keep working him with my tongue until the pulsing in my mouth has fully ceased. Only then do I loosen my grip and let him slowly slide out of me, licking his glorious dick clean as he does. Mouth now free, a chuckle escapes me. He yanks back on my hair and searches my eyes. "What's so funny, coffee boy?"

"Clouds really do taste like cotton candy."

He rolls his eyes, smiling as he lifts me up from the floor, only to throw me back onto the bed and climb on top of me. He kisses me enthusiastically, his tongue exploring my mouth. One of his arms is supporting most of his weight, the other cradling my cheek.

"Now, will you tell me what you want?" His tone is gentle as he asks, a request and not a command. It makes me want to answer. I feel my cheeks heat as I think about it. His eyebrows raise in suspicion. I bite my lip, unsure how to ask him, afraid to make this giant beautiful man on top of me uncomfortable.

"I..." I look away, trying to find the words.

He moves his hand from my cheek down to my dick, slowly stroking and using a finger to rub the wet pre-cum around my sensitive slit, all while gently kissing my neck. "Tell me, Owen. Please, coffee boy," he whispers against my collarbone.

"I want to, but..."

He looks up at me, his grey eyes intense, his hand still gripping me, making it hard to focus. His voice is warm but serious. "Owen, you can ask me for anything. I want to do everything with you."

The pleasure is building. It's getting harder and harder to think. It's now or never.

"Can I fuck you as a cloud?"

Chapter Ten
Gale

A spike of panic shoots through me. What if I can't change back? My hand stills on Owen's cock.

"What if I hurt you?"

"I know that I'm safe with you. I trust you."

"I don't know whether I trust myself. I've never done that before."

"You said you've never done any of this and so far you've been really very good at it. You're a natural." He grins at me and then cups my cheek. "Look, I want to experience every part of you, but if it makes you uncomfortable, we don't have to do it tonight or ever. You're more than enough exactly as you are."

I let my head drop on his shoulder. I want to do this with him, but I need to know that he'll be OK. What if I lose control, or for any reason can't get back to this body should things go wrong?

"Would it be better or worse if someone else was here?" I lift my head to look at him. "Not that I want anyone besides you, but in the extremely unlikely possibility someone gets hurt, there would be somebody else around to help?"

I cock my head to the side. "Better I think. But also worse."

"What's better and what's worse?"

"The safety aspect is better, but the jealousy is worse." I kiss his neck.

He laughs as he tilts his head to the side, giving me better access. "I told you, you're the only one I am interested in. We can set whatever ground rules you need to feel comfortable."

I reach down, pull out his phone from the pants on the floor, and hand it to him. Owen starts texting as I resume kissing his neck. He moans quietly and arches his body. I can't help but reach down and stroke his pretty cock.

He playfully swats my hand away. "I can't focus when you do that." His voice is breathy and needy.

"That's the point."

He moans more deeply as I resume moving my hand up and down his length, cupping his balls with my other hand. I hear the phone chirp as he sends and receives a few more messages. Owen squirms and pulls at my hair as I pick up speed, hindering his communication efforts but giving him exactly what he needs. By the time he's finished, Kyle has already agreed to help us, saying he is on his way.

As uncomfortable as I was initially with incorporating Kyle, he has made it easy since he arrived. Respectful and efficient. He listened to my concerns and easily agreed with any rules we put forth. He even asked our take on a few situations Owen and I hadn't exactly considered. The guy is... creative. I get the sense he knows what he's doing in situations like these. I'm also convinced that we could ask anything of him, and I mean *anything*, and he'd enthusiastically agree.

He seems nice enough, and now that I am convinced for certain he is not making a move on Owen, I think I can be OK with this arrangement. From what he says, he has a very open situation with several people. He also said a cloud isn't the weirdest thing he's done, but won't elaborate further. While it makes no sense for him to be this calm, his treating the situation as normal is helping me to feel more at ease.

Ground rules set, we make our way to the bathroom to turn on the shower, knowing how effective the steam was last time. I give Owen a deep kiss before turning the knob. It's a weird sensation transforming into a cloud. While technically I'm still water vapor, I seem to have more substance than an average cloud. I assume it's from whatever magic is granting me human form.

"Oh wow. You're breathtaking." Kyle stares at me, momentarily thunderstruck by my transformation. He comes to his senses and backs out of the room, taking his place in the bedroom, away from any possible danger. Until we know things are safe, he is to wait out of the strike zone, in case we need him to call for help.

Owen and I decided the living room was the best space to conduct our trial run, even setting up a few makeshift lightning rods (stainless steel cookware and unraveled coat hangers hung up around the room, grounded using extension cords - it looks like a cheap-ass science experiment) in case I lose control, which seems increasingly possible now that I see Owen walk back into the room. He's fully naked, his dick already hard and ready for me. We've talked through our options, deciding what seemed like the most possible and pleasurable, but none of us know quite for certain how this will work.

He strides right up to me, looking more confident than usual. He runs his fingers along my edge, pulling curling wisps of me through his fingers. A jolt shudders through me and he smiles. "You feel kind of tingly, warmer than I expected. I like it." He lies down, getting comfortable on the blankets and towels we've arranged on the living room floor. I hover over and begin pressing down on top of him, trying to exert weight like I have done before. "You good?" He looks at me as though I could respond. I try to show him that I am, bobbing up and down in what I hope appears like a nod. He seems satisfied, and with a soft grunt, slowly pushes his cock up into my billowy edge. "Fuck Gale, you have no idea how good this feels." He lies still, with his eyes closed, his dick fully inside of me. "God, I could stay like this forever." He slowly pulls out before thrusting back inside me. I'm surprised at how good this feels for me too, like we are closer than close. I feel myself enveloping his cock. It's not only the pressure I find pleasurable, but the feeling of moving all parts of me against him, sliding myself all over his length. I get a thrill pressing myself against him, made better by watching him take his pleasure simultaneously. He's moving so slowly, carefully savoring every moment. I condense a piece of myself into an approximation of a finger and press it against his ass, tentatively. His eyes shoot open and he freezes. Maybe I've gone too far.

He breaks out into a wild grin. "Please. Gale, I need you inside me right now." Needing no further encouragement, I push myself inside his entrance, curling to find a spot I know he'll like. He continues fucking me, and as I watch him writhe in pleasure, it's all too much and I accidentally release a bolt of lightning. It arcs out, striking one of the makeshift rods, thankfully not causing damage. Owen stills for a second, eyes wide. Shit, I've hurt him. I can feel my panic rising and another bolt forming inside me. I try to lift off him.

"Fuck babe. That was incredible. Please do that again. It felt fucking amazing." I lower myself back down and release the next bolt as he cries out. "Yes, fuck yes. Again, please." He thrusts into me wildly and I resume moving my cloud appendage in his ass.

Kyle's head peeks out of the bedroom, and taking in the scene, he grins widely at us. "Looks like everything is good. Very good." His hand reaches down to grab his clearly stiff cock, loosening his pants to whip it out, and begins stroking. The thought of someone else getting off from watching me and Owen excites me more than I ever expected. I let loose another bolt.

"Fuck, fuck, fuck. I'm not going to last much longer like this. Kyle, if you want a piece of this, you need to get over here right now." Owen slows down his thrusting, biting his lip, trying to hold himself together. It makes me want to shoot out more lightning to push him over the edge and force him to lose control.

Kyle walks over. "We're sure everyone's still good with this?" He rolls a condom over his dick as he looks down at Owen, who is looking up at me. Kyle had offered to stay in the bedroom and give us privacy, remaining only for safety, but we decided he could join in once we knew Owen was safe. I try to demonstrate my approval by stroking Owen more vigorously.

"Mmmmff. Oh, yeah, everyone's good."

Kyle slowly, uncertainly, pushes his dick into my amorphous form. "Can I just put it... Oh yep. Fuck. Yep, that's it." He freezes, just as Owen did, holding his cock fully inside me. "Oh damn, Owen. You could've warned me about the tingles." He pulls out and as he thrusts back in, I let off another crack of lightning, careful to shoot it safely away to the other side of the room.

Kyle and Owen both let out a stream of expletives. Kyle starts fucking me intensely when he hears Owen cry out that he's close. I focus on Owen, intently waiting for the moment of release. When he peaks and starts bucking under me, I let out three quick bolts of lightning in a row, causing Kyle to come immediately after. The surge of emotions and sensations, watching them fall apart around me, causes me to come myself, which I didn't even realize was possible in this form. Lightning courses through me, but I safely channel it away from the two men inside me and push the energy out in a forceful blast of plasma that sends an unfortunate frying pan flying and clattering off a far wall. My charge spent, I transform back into my human self, straddling Owen, who is still a happy shuddering mess beneath me. Kyle is leaning against the wall, trying to stay standing and looking in the direction of the frying pan, eyes large. I lean forward to kiss Owen.

"I wish I could transform for you so that you could fuck a cloud. I mean, wow. It's just not fair. Everyone should be able to experience that." He is still breathing heavily under me. I hold him, petting his head and kissing him, still riding the high of the moment.

Kyle, having regained his composure and cleaned up a bit, walks back to us with waters for each of us. His cock is in my face as he hands me my cup. "That was unique guys, really. Thank you, I've never, ever had anything like that before. Wow. But umm.. I think you need a new frying pan and probably a drywall patch."

Owen playfully shoves his shin. "That was worth a thousand frying pans. Now get your dick away from him. He's mine." Owen sits up and reaches for his water. Kyle laughs and pats me on the shoulder before taking his water into the bedroom. He emerges a couple of minutes later with his clothes on.

"It looks like you guys could use some one-on-one time. If you ever want to do that again, please don't hesitate to let me know." With a final wink, he walks out of the apartment.

Owen shrugs. "Well. He promised he wouldn't make it weird."

I pull him into a kiss.

"So now we know that if I ever need to change you back, all I have to do is fuck you." He grins at me. We both know it won't be that simple, but that doesn't mean we're not going to try.

Chapter Eleven

Owen

I stretch out my back on my blanket, looking at the passing shapes in the puffy white clouds. My storm cloud hangs back, as he always does, so I can enjoy the sight of the other clouds without rain. He always stays in sight, so I can still check him out whenever I want to, and I swear I hear him rumble each time I do.

I'm still figuring out how to date a cloud. We haven't worked out exactly *why* he shifts back into cloud form, other than that we can force it by exposing him to a lot of water. A tactic we've used to our advantage several times. The first few times he shifted unexpectedly, I lost it, which brought him back to human form quickly. That wasn't a healthy cycle for either of us, and we've worked past that now, for the most part. I trust that Gale will always return to me when he is able to.

Another fortunate discovery is that it's not just strong negative emotions that bring him back to human form, positive ones do, too. I found out my little sister got accepted to the college she had been hoping for and Gale appeared to celebrate with me.

I'm learning to appreciate the time we have together since I don't always know when he will be leaving. It's forced a change in my perspective, keeping me grounded in the present and encouraging me to give up on trying to control every moment. This new outlook, Gale's unwavering support, and all the stuff I was already doing have really helped me better manage my anxiety. I feel like I'm the best I've been in a long time.

I'm zoned out, watching Gale in the sky, so I don't even notice when someone walks over to me.

"Well now, you certainly seem to be doing better." I recognize that accent. I scramble to stand up.

"Did you...?" I glance up at Gale, unsure if I should ask about him or if that will make me sound completely unhinged. The timing of everything *could* be a coincidence, but her smile gives me the impression she knows exactly what I'm talking about. "I miss him so much. Is there any way to..." I trail off again.

"Love always finds a way, my dear." She gives me a wink, turns, and walks away.

I sit back down to think. Love finds a way? Do I love Gale? I glance up at the clouds again before looking around at the other people in the park. Families playing soccer. There's a couple on a bench near me, hands entwined. The way they look at each other, it's obvious they're in love. How can I feel so sure about a stranger, but not know for myself?

It hits me. I'm still holding back. While I trust that he will keep coming back to me for now, there's a part of me that's scared eventually he'll float away forever. That anxious part of me isn't letting me love him. But love requires boldness, it requires taking a risk. I look back up at him and whisper, "I think I love you, Gale."

As I say the words, the dark storm cloud dissipates, and a few short moments later, Gale jogs up to me, looking concerned. He searches my face, trying to figure out what emotion triggered his shift.

"Sky falling moment?" He sits down next to me.

I shake my head. "No, I think it's the opposite." I look at him. "I think I'm falling for the sky."

He smiles back at me. "That's corny as fuck." He pulls me into a kiss.

Epilogue

Gale

"You guys ready?" I stand in the bathroom waiting to hear their confirmation before I turn on the shower. There has got to be an easier way to do this, but we haven't figured it out and this works. I hear their shouted assent and turn the valve.

Transformed, I float to the living room to find Owen on hands and knees, waiting for me. Kyle waits to the side. Owen finds it hot to watch him touching me. I find it hot for him to watch Owen and me. I draw the line at him touching Owen. Owen is mine.

I move to surround Owen, pushing into his ass and wrapping myself around his cock. I've gotten much more adept at performing in my cloud form, thanks to lots of practice.

"Oh yes. Fuck, babe, that feels so good." He hangs his head down, biting his bottom lip. He was instructed not to move during this session, so his body tenses as he fights the urge to thrust into me. Watching him chew his lip and constrict all the muscles in his legs and torso, seeing him holding himself back is so hot that a bolt of lightning escapes prematurely.

Owen cries out in surprised pleasure as Kyle chuckles. "Happens to everyone, man." He moves to the side opposite Owen, getting into position before thrusting into me. "Fuck. Those little tingles get me every time." He works in and out of me, trying to hold on for what comes later.

As good as it feels to get fucked by Kyle, I focus my energy on Owen, fucking his ass and working his cock simultaneously. He was told to hold on and try to last for as long as possible. It's fucking adorable watching him try.

"It's too much, Gale, I can't," he pants, legs quivering.

"You can take it, Owen. Just a little longer and you can have his cock." Owen moans in response. Kyle keeps up his slow and steady rhythm.

I don't relent. I do everything I can to drive Owen crazy. His breathing picks up. His arms tremble. "I can't. Oh, fuck." He jerks and I release bolt after bolt of lightning as he shoots ropes of warm cum inside me. He drops to his elbows. "Holy shit. I love you so much, babe."

In a flash, I transform back into my human form, my fleshy cock swollen and ready to explode. "You ready, coffee boy?" I ask with a grin before releasing a surprised hiss as I feel Kyle spreading cold lube over my ass.

Owen shakes his head and I freeze for a second, holding my hand up for Kyle to wait, but then he turns to look at me with a sly grin. "The real question is, are you?"

"Fucking brat." I point towards the couch and he scoots over and turns to face me with a wild smile, leaning his back against it. I grab his hair, placing my other arm on the couch to support myself. "If you're going to have a mouth like that, you might as well put it to good use." I lunge forward, pressing into his open mouth with a groan. "Snap if..." He rolls his eyes, grabbing my balls with his hand, squeezing them firmly and cutting off my ability to speak for a second. "Good boy," I grunt out.

Kyle approaches behind me, grabbing my hip. "Think you can outlast Owen?" He pushes the head of his cock to my entrance, slowly sliding into me, letting me get used to him. Being a shifter has its advantages. My body adjusts quickly. He pulls back a little and then pushes a little more in careful, slow movements. He works more and more into me while Owen works magic on my balls. I've got a firm grip on his head, not letting him move on my cock, but he's doing everything he can with his talented tongue.

Kyle gets fully seated inside me before leaning to the side to look at what Owen is doing. "He really does take your cock so well, Gale." Owen looks up towards Kyle, his mouth stuffed full of cock, and releases a moan. I shake my head, hanging it over the arm supporting me.

"You both will be the death of me."

"And we're just getting started." Kyle pulls back one more time slowly before really fucking me, pounding in and out of me, the motion transferring through my ass and cock to Owen's mouth. Owen takes it well, eyes watering but focused. I feel hands moving all over my torso. My eyes are squeezed shut, trying hard to make this last, but I fail.

"Owen, I..." I can't even get out the full sentence before I explode in Owen's mouth. His hands pull me in close as he swallows me down, doing his best not to let a drop escape. Kyle thrusts a few more times before finishing himself. He gives my hips a squeeze before walking over to the bathroom to deal with the condom.

Owen drops his head back against the couch with a satisfied smile as I lean down to kiss him. I jump as something warm and wet contacts my backside. Kyle has returned with a warm washcloth to help clean me up. I turn to look at him. "You don't have to do that."

He shrugs and hands Owen another damp towel, then walks over to the bedroom to grab his clothes. He walks out a moment later, fully dressed. "Thank you, fellas. A pleasure, as always. Sometime, Gale, you gotta let me suck you off. I really like cotton candy." As he walks out, he says with a wink, "See you tomorrow, coffee boy, bright and early."

About Nicole Parker

Nicole Parker is an AuDHD 30-something California native who spends the great majority of her free time writing books, reading books, or organizing her ever-growing TBR list. She also has a spouse, some kids, and pets, but this isn't about them. Nicole's books are funny, raunchy, silly, and, most importantly, full of good vibes and happy endings.

She got into publishing in 2024 after quickly falling in love with the sentient object romance world. She took the concept of "there are no bad ideas" and really ran with it.

You can find Nicole online at:

Instagram: @nicoleparkerbooks

www.booksbynicoleparker.com

Also by Nicole

The Kyleverse Series

Weird things happen to the people around Kyle, but his go with the flow, try anything attitude usually leads to a good time. The Kyleverse is a series of sentient object romance short stories. Kyle isn't the main character, but he shows up to help the plot in one way or another. The stories are sequential but can be read as standalones.

Objectified: Kyle's Version

Kyle's whatever you need him to be, babe.
In sentient object romance, many of the encounters are considered especially unhinged. In the Kyleverse, there's one man dedicated to the pursuit of the weird. That man is Kyle. These are his stories.
Objectified: Kyle's Version tells stories you're already familiar with from Kyle's point of view, giving you a chance to really get inside his head. There are also bonus scenes that you haven't

read before, so you can finally find out what else he was up to while "off the page."

This book is a companion piece to Objectified: Kyleverse Books 1-10. It's recommended to read the main series prior to Kyle's Version as there's no time for character introductions (except when they pop up in surprising places, IYKYK). Enjoy this as a collection of complimentary stories, rather than a singular overarching plot.

Kyleverse Holiday Specials

Shift

Shift is a Halloween special in the Kyleverse, a series of sentient object romance short stories. Kyle isn't the main character, but he shows up to help the plot in one way or another. This story contains characters from the main series. For the best experience, it is recommended to read Rake prior to reading Shift, as the main characters are the same. There are mentions of characters from Faulty as well.

Heat

Heat is a friendsgiving special in the Kyleverse, a series of sentient object romance short stories. Kyle isn't the main character, but he shows up to help the plot in one way or another. This story contains characters from the main series. For the best experience, it is recommended to read Spread prior to reading

Shift, as the main characters are the same. There are mentions of characters from Rake and Licked as well.

My Date with an Ampersand

Faced with yet another late night at the library, graphemics student Gwen Lettiere is at her wit's end. For months, she's been researching the mystery of the ampersand to no avail.

But she's not the only one hiding in the stacks. Sandy has been watching Gwen from the shadows, fostering an obsession with the beautiful researcher. No one has cared for Sandy since she was denounced as a letter almost 200 years ago, so when she accidentally reveals herself to Gwen, she shoots her shot.

After a very hot study session, Gwen discovers there is a more sinister side to Sandy's history than what's written in the history books. When the harsh reality of discrimination puts Sandy in danger, Gwen refuses to let her stand-alone.

Can the two of them really take on twenty-six adversaries and live to tell the tale?

My Date With the Ampersand is part of The Sentient Object Holiday Series, a shared series curated by some of your favorite off-the-wall authors: Biblio Barbie, Dakota Cockaday, Holly Wilde, Luna Cantrip, Nicole Parker, Sylvia Morrow, Thea Masen, Unfortunate Reads, and Vera Valentine. It is meant for readers 18 and over who are ready to embrace a deeper experience with some unusual holidays.

Fully Charged: A Parody Sentient Object Romance

Cowritten with Unfortunate Reads

Jewel is a newly single mom who just wants to unwind in her rare time alone. The kids are away, and it's time for mama to play...with herself.

Except the off-brand batteries in her favorite tool die mid-session. When she replaces them with the industry leader, Ohm-azing, Jewel gets more than long lasting pleasure. Wattson has been sent from Ohm-azing headquarters to ensure Jewel is 100% satisfied.

Fully Charged is a parody sentient object romance intended for audiences over 18 years old. This contains intimate relations between a human woman and a mythical pink rabbit. Read at your own risk!

Santa's Sack

Cowritten with Unfortunate Reads

Last year, disaster struck when Santa Claus was kidnapped and taken to Halloweenville. This year, the Seasonal Symposium Officials are putting protective measures in place.

Except...

Santa and his captor, Sackman, inadvertently discovered they shared dark carnal proclivities. They will do whatever it takes to ensure a repeat performance this year, but will just one night be enough?

No one expects Santa to beg to be on the naughty list.

Santa's Sack is a parody (sentient object adjacent) romance intended for audiences over 18 years old. This story contains intimate relations between a sack/man and Santa. Check interior content considerations for a full list of information, and read at your own risk!

Made in the USA
Las Vegas, NV
17 May 2025

22302340R00038